Please checkout our latest
publications here on the website:
http://www.clivebritton.co.uk

Thank you so much for taking the time to
give the comic a spin.
Please could I ask you to write
a short review. Just click on the comic on
the Amazon book-shelf, and scroll down
to the reviews window.

Acknowledgements

This book is dedicated to the power of friendship.
The characters within are based on real people, and by that, I mean
no bullshit, down-to-earth people who look out for one another.
I dedicate this to all of you.
I love you all.

The Swan

Pubs like The Swan are a dying breed.
Once the beating heart of every community, these little
haunts were the backbones of our society.

Sadly, our pubs are on the decline. The government
don't want you talking to one another.

Well done, Valerie, for looking after the place
with such duty, commitment, and love.

Keep the flame burning, people.

The Swan
and the hole
in the universe

Double hard, bastards at The Bull.

It was in a creepy little
town called
Crawley, that a
strange happening
occurred.

In a a little pub where
Val, the Landlady
would stand for
no nonsense.

It wasn't like the other pubs
in the town, where grown men
argued over conundrums such
as how old the carpet is.

The Pub garden.

The typical cheerful mood
of The Swan
was darkened when
Will, the lead singer of The Gas
revealed what had happened
to Kosta, and The
Fortune Tellers.

You see...
The Gas, and The
Fortune Tellers, had travelled
the same path;
they were cut
from the same cloth.

The Fortune Tellers, and The Gas

"Kosta hasn't
been seen for a while,"
Will explained.

"What I witnessed last
night has shocked me to my core,"
he confessed.

"One minute they were playing
'Seaside Town,'
and the next; they were gone!"

When Will awoke.

Worried for his friends safety,
Will sort the help of a noble
woman, and told her what
he had seen.

Amazed by the story Will had
disclosed, the noble woman said...
"So you are telling me that
Kosta has been sucked
into another world?"

"Yes," Will replied.
"And possibly The Fortune
Tellers as well!"

Kosta being kidnapped.

"Well...!" the noble woman exclaimed. "I've heard it all now!"

But, the more Will tried to explain, the more incredible the story sounded.

"They are being sucked into another dimension," he insisted.

The Swan

"Another dimension?" Angus
gasped.
"Is that the place where
the sane people live?"

"There is a hole in the
fabric of our universe,"
Will educated.
"And it's right outside the door!"

One of the Swan's locals rested
his pint on the bar, and
stepped forward.
"Have you tried approaching
the local council?"
he asked.

The local Council.

"Are you kidding?"
Will exclaimed, whilst trying
not to laugh.
"Those Wankers can't
even fix
the holes in the roads!"

"Why not ask one of the
fortune tellers?" another
of the regulars
suggested.

Zelda The Wise.

"Zelda is the lady who you seek!"
One of the elders suggested.
"She is the wisest woman
in all the universes."

"No way," Will replied.
she scares me
to death!"

"What about Celeste?"
another of the elders proposed.
He tapped her name into
his phone, and
her image appeared.

Celeste.

The men of the Swan
formed a posse, and
marched over to The White Hart.

"You are searching for
your friends,"
the Teller told, as she gazed
down at the cards.

The White Hart fell
silent as Celeste
revealed the secrets
of the cards.

Fading from existence.

Now, there's a good name for a band!

"Your friends are fading
from existence,"
the Tarot reader
explained.

"Another band from another
realm feed on their
energy."

"I knew it!"
Will declared.
"How can we get them
back?"

Magic-mushroom, and frog's legs smoothie.

The Tarot reader instructed
the men to mix a potion
of psilocybin and
frog's legs.

"But, be aware," she warned.
"Dark forces await you."

On the bar stood a potion
so toxic, even the band
from the other side
of the universe
were sickened at the
thought of downing it.

Slider.

"Slider is the front man of
a band called the Vampires,"
Celeste revealed.
"Probably the best band
in all the Universes."

"Utter Bollocks,"
Will rejected.
"Stand aside!
I'm going to get Kosta!"

"It maybe too late"
Celeste warned.
for Kosta's heart has
been enticed!"

The woman who enticed Kosta's heart.

Will drank down the psilocybin, and frog's legs potion in one, and prepared himself for the road."

A storm had broken outside. A torrent of water swelled like a river as it carried everything in its wake down the tiny cobbled street outside The Swan.

Will thundering through the gap in the universe.

Will gathered his coat,
and tore through the fabric
to the other side.

Celeste guided Will to the
band, but The Fortune Tellers
had already been
consumed
by the spell.

Gig at The Old Stout House.

"What's the matter with
you lot?"
Will questioned
when he stepped into
The Old Stout House.

"It was the psilocybin,
and frog's legs potion,
that done it,"
the barman revealed.

"I'll have two of them, then
please, Barman."

The other side of the universe.

And, so it was
that Will had entered another
dimension.

"Keep that door open,"
Jambo shouted as he ran
towards the light.

"Where's this Slider bloke?"
Will asked.

Slider awaiting Will's arrival.

"We should have a battle
of the bands!"
Slider suggested.

"The Fortune Tellers
against
The Vampires!"

"It will be the
greatest party in
the cosmos."

The greatest party in the cosmos.

"If the Fortune Tellers
win, I will close
the gap in the universe
and you will never hear from
us again,"
Slider promised.

"What about Kosta?"
Will asked.

"For Kosta,
it may already be too late,
for his heart is tempted
by a beautiful woman."

The beautiful woman.

"Kosta has been lured
into our dimension
by a beautiful, alluring woman,"

"I'm afraid the band
will have to cope
without him."

But, without Kosta,
there could be no band!

Cosmic dual.

And the battle began.

The guitarists
unleashed some of the most
cosmic solos ever known
to any of
the universes.

The drummers thrashed
out the most
intoxicating beats.

Space dust.

Musicians from every corner
of each universe,
played like their souls
depended on it.

It was the craziest gig
The Swan had ever known,
apart from
every other Tuesday.

Open mic at The Swan.

Suddenly,
the bell rang.

"Last orders at the bar, please!"

Did the Fortune Tellers
win the battle?

What happened to Will?

Have the pot holes been repaired?

And what became of Kosta?

Find out in The Swan's next
adventure.

Thank you so much for making it this far.

I greatly appreciate the time you took to give the comic a spin. As a small indie publisher, it means a lot and I hope I am making a difference in your journey.

If you have a few spare minutes, could I ask that you leave feedback on Amazon; it would mean a lot. I would love to hear about your experience.

http://www.clivebritton.co.uk

To leave your feedback:
Go to the Amazon bookshelf, tap in Clive Britton, tap on the comic, and scroll down to the reviews window.
Thanks again.

Printed in Great Britain
by Amazon

41479250R00031